Bugs Bunny™
and the Health Hog

By Teddy Slater
Illustrated by Darrell Baker

A GOLDEN BOOK • NEW YORK
Western Publishing Company, Inc., Racine, Wisconsin 53404

Copyright © 1986 Warner Bros. Inc. All rights reserved. Printed in the U.S.A. by Western Publishing Company, Inc.
No part of this book may be reproduced or copied in any form without written permission from the publisher.
GOLDEN®, GOLDEN & DESIGN®, A GOLDEN BOOK®, and A LITTLE GOLDEN BOOK® are trademarks
of Western Publishing Company, Inc.
Library of Congress Catalog Card Number: 85-51674 ISBN 0-307-01100-3   C D E F G H I J
BUGS BUNNY is the trademark of Warner Bros. Inc. used under license.

After seven straight days of rain, Bugs Bunny was getting bored just sitting around his burrow.

"I need to get some exercise," Bugs thought.

So he grabbed his galoshes and umbrella and headed for town to join a health club.

"We're having a special sale this week," the man at the Hillsdale Health Club told Bugs. "Ask a friend to sign up with you, and get an extra three months' membership free."

That sounded like a great deal to Bugs. He quickly set off to find his best buddy, Porky Pig.

"Eh, what's up, doc?" Bugs asked when he reached Porky's house. "You look a little down."

"I'm bored," said Porky. "It's this awful rain."

"I know just what you need," Bugs said. And he told Porky all about the health club.

Porky hesitated, but Bugs insisted. "You know, pal," Bugs said, "you've been looking even porkier than usual lately. You should lose a few pounds."

Finally Porky agreed to give it a try.

The next day, the two friends signed up at the health club. They started off with an aerobics class, exercising to the beat of a jazzy dance tune. But while everyone else struggled to keep up with the instructor...

...Porky found his mind wandering!

After aerobics, they jumped into the pool. But while
Bugs churned through the water like a speedy torpedo...

...Porky found his mind wandering again!

On the way home after their workout, though, Porky had to admit that he felt surprisingly refreshed.

"This is just the beginning," Bugs said. "Believe me, the more you work out, the better you'll feel."

Bugs soon began to regret those words.

Day by day, Porky became more and more involved in exercising. He began arriving at the club earlier than Bugs, and leaving later. He didn't even take a break for lunch. Porky was too busy exercising to think about anything else.

Bugs felt sad—and lonely. He missed his friend.

SNACKS

One night, Bugs heard a knock at his door. He looked
up and saw two little pink feet. "It's Porky!" he thought
hopefully.

But when he opened the door, he saw Porky's
girlfriend, Petunia Pig, standing there. She looked upset.

"I need to talk to you," Petunia said to Bugs.

"Go ahead," Bugs urged. "I'm all ears."

"What have you done to Porky?" she cried. "He told me you think he's too fat. Now he never wants to go out to dinner because he's on a diet. And he's usually too tired to go out at night. I hardly ever see him anymore. I miss him."

"I know," Bugs said guiltily. "I do, too. But don't worry. I'll fix this mess."

The next day, Bugs saw Porky in the locker room.

"I was wrong about you," Bugs said. "You *should* be plump. Like the old sayings go, 'Quick as a bunny,' 'Wise as an owl,' and, er, let's face it—'Fat as a pig'!

"You haven't been yourself since you joined this club," Bugs went on. "Soon I won't even be able to recognize you. Besides, I really miss you."

Porky shook his head doubtfully. "You're right, Bugs," he said. "I haven't been much of a friend. But you were right before, too. I *am* too fat. I promise to cut down on my workouts—just as soon as I lose a few more pounds. Okay?"

"Oh, Porky!" Bugs cried. "How can I convince you that you're fine just as you are?"

Then Bugs Bunny came up with a plan. The next morning, he showed up at the club even earlier than Porky. He sneaked into the gym with a can of silver paint and changed the number on one of the weights from 10 to 20.

When Porky Pig arrived later and began pumping iron, he could hardly believe his progress.

"Look, Bugs," Porky cried. "Last week I couldn't get the ten-pound weight off the ground, and now I'm lifting twice that."

"Great," Bugs said. "Now you won't need to work out so much anymore."

Porky patted his tummy. "No," he said, "I may be getting stronger, but I'm still as fat as ever."

Bugs was discouraged—but he wouldn't give up!

He decided to swipe a pair of Porky's sweatpants from his gym bag. He took them over to Petunia's and asked her to let out the waistband.

"I hope this works," Bugs told Petunia.

When Porky put on the sweatpants the next day, he noticed nothing wrong…until he started lifting his weights!

"Wow!" Bugs exclaimed. "You really have lost a lot of weight. Now you can stop dieting and exercising, and we can have some real fun."

"Oh, no," Porky said. "I'm still a little too fat."

That week, the carnival came to town. Bugs asked Porky to leave the club early and go over to the fairground, but Porky didn't want to miss his afternoon calisthenics class.

So Bugs went to the carnival alone. While passing by the magic mirrors in the Fun House, he had a real brainstorm.

Bright and early the next morning, Bugs hung a magic mirror on Porky's locker door. Then he slipped out into the hall to see what would happen next.

When Porky opened his locker and took a look in the mirror, he squealed at what he saw.

Bugs strolled over to Porky. "Eh, what's up, doc?" he asked casually.

"You were right!" Porky cried. "Look at what I've done to myself with all this silly dieting and exercising. Why, I look a hundred times worse than I did at my very fattest. I never should have joined this awful club!"

"That's not true," Bugs said. "There's nothing silly about exercising or dieting—in moderation. But you overdid it. You turned into a health hog, and there's nothing healthy about that!"

"Gee, I'd give anything to be my old self again," Porky said glumly.

Porky looked so sad that Bugs knew he'd learned his lesson. He told Porky about the tricks he'd played.

"So you see," Bugs concluded, "you still *are* your old self."

"Oh, boy!" Porky said. "Let's celebrate!" He called
Petunia and asked her to join them at the snack bar.

Bugs ordered carrot cake and carrot juice for everyone.

"Here's to physical fitness—in moderation!" Porky said,
lifting his glass.

"And here's to friendship," Bugs added. He gave his
pal a big grin. And Petunia gave him a big hug.